D1153058

THE GREATEST ADVENTURES IN THE WORLD

ROBIN HOOD
and the
SILVER
ARROW

TONY BRADMAN & TONY ROSS

ORCHARD BOOKS

ORCHARD BOOKS
96 Leonard Street, London EC2A 4XD
Orchard Books Australia
32/45-51 Huntley Street, Alexandria, NSW 2015
ISBN 1 84362 468 0 (hardback)
ISBN 1 84362 474 5 (paperback)
The text was first published in Great Britain in the form of a gift collection called
Swords, Sorcerers and Superheroes with full colour illustrations by Tony Ross, in 2003
This edition first published in hardback in 2004
First paperback publication in 2005
Text © Tony Bradman 2003
Illustrations © Tony Ross 2004
The rights of Tony Bradman to be identified as the author and of Tony Ross
to be identified as the illustrator of this work have been asserted by them
in accordance with the Copyright, Designs and Patents Act, 1988.
A CIP catalogue record for this book is available from the British Library.
1 3 5 7 9 10 8 6 4 2 (hardback)
1 3 5 7 9 10 8 6 4 2 (paperback)
Printed in Great Britain
www.wattspublishing.co.uk

CONTENTS

CHAPTER ONE

THE NORMAN INVADERS

TIMES WERE TOUGH IN
England in the years after the
Norman invaders came. They conquered
the whole country with fire and sword,
they robbed and killed and looted and
pillaged, and they took the best of

everything for themselves, especially
the farmland. Then they settled down to
rule over the ordinary people – the
Saxons – with violence and cruelty
and scorn.

Few dared stand against their might,
and those that did rebel were soon
crushed, all except one…a young man
the people knew as Robin Hood.

Some said that Robin was really Robert of Locksley, the son of a Saxon noble, and that his father had been murdered by some Norman knights so that they could seize his land. Others said Robin was the son of a poor hunter, or a yeoman farmer's son who had been set upon by a gang of Norman soldiers for no reason – and had left three of them dead before making his escape.

Whatever the truth, Robin had long ago been declared an outlaw, and had taken refuge in the depths of Sherwood Forest, an ancient wood that stood near the city of Nottingham. There he gathered a band of faithful followers – boys and men, and some girls and women too – many of whom had seen their homes burned and their entire families slaughtered before their eyes.

8

But Robin and his followers – his band of outlaws, as he called them – did a lot more than just hide. They struck back, hard and often, swooping on columns of Norman soldiers who strayed near the forest, killing dozens in a hail of arrows, then silently returning into the darkness between the trees. They held up Norman travellers as well, robbing the rich to give to the poor.

CHAPTER TWO

ROBIN AND THE SHERIFF OF NOTTINGHAM

THE SAXONS ADORED ROBIN, and wherever the people gathered they told each other news of his latest escapades. They were proud of his daring and his boldness, his sense of humour and his fighting skills – many of the outlaws

11

were fine archers, Will Scarlett being
particularly good – but Robin was said to
be the best shot with a longbow in
England. And somehow just knowing
Robin was standing up for them seemed to
keep the people going.

The Normans, of course, feared and
hated Robin Hood in equal measure.

One Norman in particular – the Sheriff of Nottingham, the local overlord, a brutal and cunning man – grew ever more determined to catch Robin and end his mischief once and for all.

But no matter how many expeditions he sent against Robin, no matter how many men he set to guard travellers on the road, he could no more catch Robin Hood than seize a handful of mist.

So the sheriff brooded in his great grim stone castle, wondering what he could do. And eventually he devised a plan that he thought might work.

One dark evening, a young boy – the son of one of the outlaws – ran into a clearing deep in the heart of Sherwood Forest, the secret hideaway of Robin and his band. They were sitting round a campfire, eating their evening meal – venison from a deer that belonged to the Sheriff of Nottingham. Robin always said poaching deer from the sheriff made it taste even better.

"Robin!" said the boy, skidding to a halt before him. "Have a look at this! It was pinned to the door of a tavern, and there are more all over the place!"

The boy eagerly held out a piece of parchment to Robin, who took it from him and read what was written on it. Then Robin smiled, and looked up.

"Listen to this, lads," he said, and the outlaws grew quiet. "It seems our old friend the Sheriff of Nottingham is in need of entertainment – he wants to find the best bowman in England, so he's holding an archery contest at the castle. There's a rich prize for the man who wins, too – a silver arrow."

"But…you're not seriously thinking of entering, are you, Robin?" said Marian, Robin's sweetheart, a worried expression on her face. "It's a trap."

15

"Marian's right, Robin," said Will Scarlett, who'd been with him since the earliest days in Sherwood. "He knows you're the best archer in England…"

"And he knows you can't resist a challenge," said Friar Tuck, another longstanding band member. "So it's just a crafty way of flushing you out."

One by one, the other outlaws – Much the Miller's son, Little John, Alan A'Dale and the rest – joined in, each of them saying the same thing, all of them worried for their leader. The clearing was filled with the noise of their voices, until at last Robin held up his hands and quietened them down again.

"Of course it's a trap," said Robin, still smiling in the flickering firelight. "I know that as well as any of you. All the more reason to go – and beat it."

"But what good will it do to put yourself in such danger?" said Marian. "You're the people's only hope, the only thing that keeps them going…"

"Exactly!" said Robin, grinning now. "So think how they'll feel if I can beat the sheriff at his own game, if I can tweak his beard in front of them!"

"Ah, since you put it like that…" murmured Friar Tuck, eyes twinkling.

The other outlaws were glancing at each other, several of them starting to smile too. Marian, however, looked as if she needed more convincing.

"I'm not sure, Robin," she said, frowning at him. "I think it's too risky."

"For heaven's sake, Marian, just being a Saxon these days is pretty risky!" laughed Robin. The outlaws laughed with him, and Marian smiled. "At least this way we might have some fun," Robin added. "Anyway, trust me – I'll come up with a plan. The sheriff isn't the only one who can be cunning…"

CHAPTER THREE

THE ARCHERY CONTEST

A WEEK LATER, THE DAY OF THE archery contest dawned bright and sunny, and a great crowd began to gather in the main courtyard of the sheriff's castle. The Saxon people – who needed some entertainment themselves – were

kept to one side, penned in behind
a barrier, and watched by a line of
hard-faced Norman soldiers in their
iron helmets and chain-mail – their
swords drawn.

A special pavilion – a gaudy thing of
bright silks and fluttering pennants – had
been set up for the sheriff at the far end of
the courtyard, so he could have the best
view of the contest, and also be protected
from the glare of the sun. He sat in a
chair as big as a king's throne, on a raised
platform flanked by his bodyguard,
and surrounded by rich, local
Normans and their wives.

A low table stood in
front of the sheriff, and
the silver arrow lay on it.

"I trust our men have been told to stay vigilant," the sheriff muttered to the captain of the guard, who was standing beside him. "And that they're to ensure – on pain of their own deaths – that the man we want doesn't escape."

"Don't worry, my lord, they've all been fully briefed," the captain replied, smiling. "This is going to be a day to remember! By the way, two of the guard have said they want to enter the contest themselves. Do they have your permission?"

"Yes, yes," the sheriff hissed irritably,
and waved the captain away.

The sheriff, in fact, was feeling rather
tense, and kept scanning the faces in the
crowd, wondering if
one of them might be his
arch-enemy, the shadowy
Saxon outlaw who had
caused him so much trouble.
The sheriff had never seen
Robin Hood, so he had no
idea what he looked like.
No one had even been able to
give the sheriff a description of him.

At last the sheriff summoned his herald
and told him to get things moving. The
herald blew his trumpet, and the
competitors marched out.

They lined up before the sheriff, and the herald explained the rules of the contest. The sheriff leaned forward to study the competitors more closely, knowing already that more than a hundred men from all over the country had come to try and win the silver arrow. He could see now that they were mostly Saxons, some young, a few old, the rest of them ordinary-looking Saxon peasants, except for the two Norman guards the captain had mentioned, who stood apart.

Only one of the contestants seemed to stand out, the sheriff thought, and that was a sturdy fellow, dressed from head to foot in Lincoln green – and with the hood of his tunic raised so no one could see his face. "Umm, very suspicious," thought the sheriff, narrowing his eyes and rubbing his chin. He decided this mysterious, hooded archer might well be the man to watch.

Then, with another blast from the herald's trumpet, the contest began. The targets had been set up against the castle wall, at a distance of fifty paces for the first round.

The archers stepped forward, one by one, to take their shots, the crowd loudly enjoying themselves, the sheriff and his men silently watching the proceedings like hawks.

Half the competitors were quickly eliminated, the targets moved back a further twenty-five paces, and so on.

Soon there were ten competitors, with the target at a hundred and twenty-five paces, then five archers with the target at a hundred and fifty paces, and all five were very good. Two of them were the Norman soldiers who had entered the contest, which gave the sheriff some satisfaction – at least it showed the Saxons that Normans could be good archers too, although the crowd booed every time they took a shot.

The other three were Saxons, two of them fine archers, but the third had easily been the best bowman of all during the contest so far – and he was none other than the mysterious hooded man.

He hit the centre of the target every time, and never lowered his hood or seemed to speak.

The sheriff glanced now at the captain of his bodyguard, and nodded slightly at him.

The captain turned to whisper an order to one of his men, and soon more Norman soldiers appeared from behind the pavilion. They moved forward and stood behind the five competitors, the bright sunlight glinting off their iron helmets and their swords. The captain looked at the sheriff, but the sheriff gave him a signal that obviously meant he should wait a little...

Meanwhile, the contest was entering its final phase. The two Saxons took their last shots, which were fine, but not good enough to win. Then the two Normans took their shots, which were of much the same standard. And then the mysterious, hooded man stepped forward. A hush fell over the castle courtyard, everyone holding their breath as he raised his great longbow.

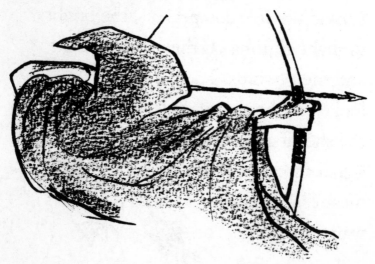

He pulled back the string, aimed – and
let fly, the arrow swishing through the air
and THUDDING into the dead centre
of the target, the best shot of the day.
The Saxon crowd cheered happily...but
then things happened fast.

"Hold that man!" yelled the
sheriff, who could remain
patient no longer.

The waiting soldiers
did just that, grabbing the
mysterious hooded man and
holding him by the arms. The
crowd murmured in confusion, then began
to boo, but the sheriff took no notice. He
leapt up from his seat and strode over to
the soldiers and the contestants, the
captain hurrying behind him.

"My lord," the captain said breathlessly, "I think you should know that—"

"Not now, you idiot!" the sheriff snapped, irritably waving him away again. The sheriff walked on, stopping eventually in front of the hooded man, who stood between his Norman captors with his head down.

"So, Robin Hood," he said, practically spitting out the name, "we meet at last." And with that the sheriff roughly pulled back the man's hood to reveal a smiling young face. "Well, what do you have to say?" snarled the sheriff.

"Not much," said the young man. "Except that I am not the one you seek."

30

"Hah!" snorted the sheriff. "You're just trying to save your skin. Guards, take the wretch away. We'll hang him later – after we've tortured him…"

"Not so fast there, lads!" said one of the two Norman soldiers who had competed in the contest. "He's telling the truth. He isn't Robin Hood."

"What are you talking about, man?" the sheriff spluttered furiously, his face red with anger. "How can you possibly know whether he is or he isn't?"

"Because his name is Will Scarlett," said
the soldier, removing his helmet. "I am
Robin Hood. And now it's time to end
this contest. Seize him, Alan!"

Suddenly the other Norman
contestant whipped out a
dagger and moved forward.
Before anyone could
stop him, he grabbed
the sheriff and held
the dagger to his throat,
the point pressing into
the skin. The crowd
howled, and the
sheriff's men were dazed
and confused, not knowing what to do.
"Don't just stand there, you fools!" the
sheriff yelled. "Kill them!"

"I wouldn't do that, if I were you, lads," said Robin, and smiled at them. "One false move, and I promise you that my friend Alan here will cut the sheriff a brand new windpipe. In fact, you'd better all drop your weapons. And if you want another reason for doing that, have a look around you!"

The captain and his men did as Robin said, and saw figures suddenly appearing on the castle walls and emerging from the crowd – outlaws from Robin's band, each one carrying a bow with an arrow aimed at a Norman heart. Several of the contestants stepped forward and joined Robin too.

The captain and his men dropped their weapons with a clatter.

"I'm very sorry, my lord," said the captain. "But I was trying to tell you, we found a couple of the men stripped of their uniforms and tied up…"

"All part of the plan, Sheriff," said Robin. "And not a bad fit, either."

Then Robin turned to address the crowd. "The sheriff thought he could trap me, Robin Hood, by setting up this contest," he said, his voice ringing loud and clear. "But it looks like we've managed to spoil his day, don't you think?"

The crowd roared its appreciation, and Robin and his outlaws smiled.

"Bah!" snorted the sheriff. "If you are Robin Hood, then the stories about your archery can't be true. You were beaten in the contest fair and square."

"Is that so?" said Robin. He knew the sheriff was trying to belittle him in front of the crowd. "Well, perhaps I'd better give everybody here a taste of what I can really do. You don't mind if I have another shot, do you, Will?"

"Be my guest, Robin," said Will. "But mine is a hard shot to beat."

Robin didn't reply. He raised his bow, took an arrow from his quiver and fitted it to the string. He slowly drew the arrow back until its tail feathers rested on his cheek. He aimed at the target, the one with Will's last arrow still sticking out of its centre. And once more the crowd – in fact everybody in the courtyard, Norman and Saxon, rich and poor alike – held its breath.

Robin stood for several seconds, bow

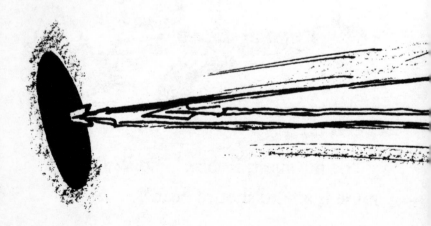

poised, the sun shining on him.

Then he released the string, and his arrow flew straight and true through the air…and split Will's arrow right down the middle, THWACKING into exactly the same spot at the very centre of the target. A great cheer went up from the crowd, and even the Normans were impressed, the sheriff's jaw falling open in amazement against Alan A'Dale's arm round his throat.

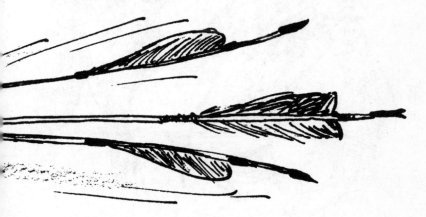

"Well, that ought to prove who I am, and no mistake," said Robin. "And I think a shot like that deserves a rich prize – don't you, Sheriff? Will, fetch me that silver arrow while I find out where Marian's got to with the horses."

Will went to collect the silver arrow
from where it lay on the table in front of
the pavilion, and Robin pulled a hunting
horn from beneath his chainmail. He blew
three loud blasts on it, and soon Marian
came cantering through the castle gates
on a tall horse, leading four more behind
her, and rode up to him. She was wearing
Lincoln green and had a bow slung across
her back.

"I take it everything's gone to plan then, Robin?" she said, and smiled.

"Oh yes, Marian," Robin replied, swinging into the saddle of one of the spare horses. "Now it's time to head for home. I'm afraid you're coming too, Sheriff," he added. "At least as far as the edge of the forest, anyway. But it's a lovely day for a ride in the country. I'm sure you'll enjoy it."

Will got the sheriff on to one of the
horses and tied his hands to the saddle.
Then they mounted, and Robin led them
past the cheering crowd and towards the
gate, holding the silver arrow above his
head in triumph, Marian beside him.
Once outside, they broke into a gallop,
hooves thundering as they made for
Sherwood Forest in the distance.

And inside the castle, the other outlaws faded away like ghosts in the sunlight before the Normans managed to pull themselves together and do anything...

CHAPTER FOUR

THE SHERIFF'S
EMBARRASSMENT

A FEW HOURS LATER THE
sheriff returned, still tied to a horse,
sitting backwards on it, but minus all his
clothes! The Saxon people thought it was
the funniest thing they'd ever seen, and
the story soon travelled round England,

along with the tale of everything else that had happened that day.

Robin's fight against the Normans wasn't over, of course. It went on for many more years, and he and the Sheriff of Nottingham had other encounters, although the sheriff's reputation never recovered from this first one. Robin's fame grew and grew, though, and to this day, wherever poor people fight against tyranny, his name is remembered and the stories about him told.

But this story's at an end. So let's leave Robin and his band of outlaws, sitting round their campfire surrounded by the dark of Sherwood Forest, the sound of their talk and laughter rising to the branches above their heads.

ROBIN HOOD
Outlaw with a Sense of Humour

By Tony Bradman

Nobody knows if there was a real Robin Hood, although many historians have tried their best to track one down. All we can be sure of is that the stories about a character bearing this name seem to have their roots in early thirteenth century England, and that over the centuries Robin Hood has become one of the most popular legendary figures in the world.

Why do these tales have such appeal? To begin with, Robin's cause is just. He's a hero, fighting the wicked and the strong on behalf of the weak and the powerless. In some versions of the stories he's a persecuted Saxon himself; in others, he's a young noble unfairly denied his inheritance. But whether he's a peasant or an aristocrat, we know that he's right and that the villainous Normans are wrong. So naturally we're always on Robin's side.

Then there's the life Robin leads, the exciting

existence of an outlaw. He doesn't have to go to school or work, or do any of the boring things that make up most people's lives. He spends his time with his friends – his Merry Men – in the forest, hunting the king's deer and having lots of adventures. Of course there's danger, too, but that only adds spice to the mixture!

Robin is also pretty cool. He's brave and bold, a terrific archer and fighter. But one of his greatest weapons is his sense of humour. He loves to trick his enemies, to make them look stupid in front of the people they oppress. Cheekiness is always popular in a hero wherever in the world their story might come from. That young scamp Aladdin from *The Thousand and One Nights*, the great collection of Arabic, Persian and Indian tales, is another example – he's brave and clever, but he's funny as well. In fact, Robin is the ancestor of many heroes in books and films – Zorro, the Scarlet Pimpernel, Asterix, Batman – anyone who fights for the weak and delivers a funny line as he beats the baddies yet again.

That's why we like Aladdin and Robin Hood – and why Robin Hood's story will be around for ever.

ORCHARD MYTHS AND CLASSICS

THE GREATEST ADVENTURES IN THE WORLD

TONY BRADMAN & TONY ROSS

Ali Baba and the Stolen Treasure	1 84362 473 7
Jason and the Voyage to the Edge of the World	1 84362 472 9
Robin Hood and the Silver Arrow	1 84362 474 5
Aladdin and the Fabulous Genie	1 84362 477 X
Arthur and the King's Sword	1 84362 475 3
William Tell and the Apple for Freedom	1 84362 476 1

All priced at £3.99

Orchard Myths and Classics are available from all good bookshops,or can be ordered
direct from the publisher: Orchard Books, PO BOX 29, Douglas IM99 1BQ
Credit card orders please telephone 01624 836000
or fax 01624 837033or visit our Internet site: www.wattspub.co.uk
or e-mail: bookshop@enterprise.net for details.

To order please quote title, author and ISBN
and your full name and address.
Cheques and postal orders should be made payable to 'Bookpost plc.'
Postage and packing is FREE within the UK
(overseas customers should add £1.00 per book).

Prices and availability are subject to change.